The Little Christmas Tree

A tale of growing and becoming

by
Janie Jasin

♥

illustrated by
Pam Kurtz

SCHOLASTIC INC.
New York Toronto London Auckland Sydney
Mexico City New Delhi Hong Kong

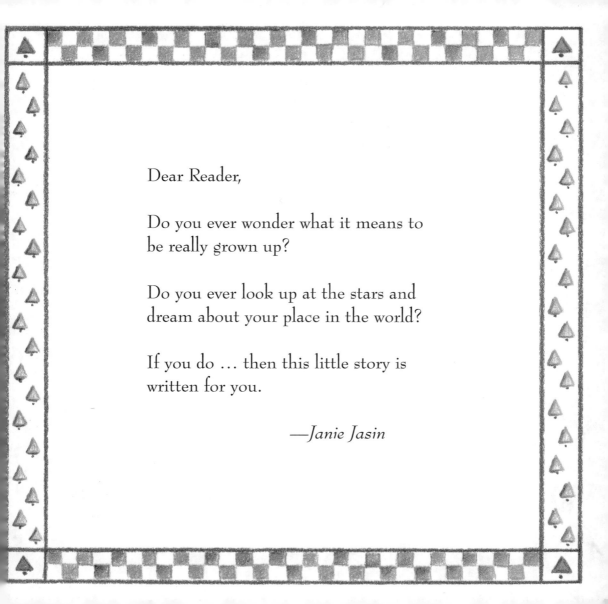

Dear Reader,

Do you ever wonder what it means to be really grown up?

Do you ever look up at the stars and dream about your place in the world?

If you do … then this little story is written for you.

—*Janie Jasin*

Dedicated
to
The Master Creator,
Maker of All the Trees
and All the Children
in the World

nce upon a time in a field of young Christmas tree seedlings, there stood a tiny tree, smaller than all of the other seedlings. The little tree stood attentively in her row, planted in the soft, sandy soil among the other little trees.

This littlest tree wanted to grow tall enough to become a real Christmas tree.

As she was growing, the littlest tree decided to think about all the things that made her happy.

The first thing she thought of was the Sun.

"I love the Sunshine, so warm on my green branches," she said to herself, "I can feel it helping me grow tall all summer long."

The littlest tree tipped her head and thought some more.

"And the Sky, I love that, too. I watch it each day as it changes, some days all cloudy and grey and some days so clear and blue."

Then she felt a gentle breeze begin to rustle through her tiny green needles.

"The Wind! I can't forget the Wind. When I hear the Wind coming, I listen very carefully and scrunch myself down as low as I can to let it blow through me. I can feel it all the way from my most top branch to my very lowest branches."

The littlest tree thought and thought about the many wonderful things in her world.

"Of course, there's the Rain. How delicious it feels on my needles, so soft and warm, smelling sweetly of grass and earth."

"I know I'm lucky to have the Rain — and the Sun and the Sky and the Wind. They care for me and help me grow tall. But I do wish I would grow faster."

And the littlest tree waited and dreamed about becoming a Christmas tree.

Sometimes the littlest tree leaned over to listen to the grown-up trees talking to each other in the nearby woods. She learned that when she grew taller, trimmers would come with their clippers to carefully shape her tree form.

"I won't be afraid when the trimmers come," she told herself. "I know that I will be shaped to become a beautiful Christmas tree with my very tip top reaching high toward the Heavens."

"Christmas trees must be a lot like people," thought the littlest tree. "People who are good and strong look up to the Heavens for strength and encouragement. I will look up and stand patiently until I am tall enough to be chosen for Christmas."

She called out to the Sky, "Please, choose me! I am ready for a Christmas celebration. I am ready for the season of Lights and Life."

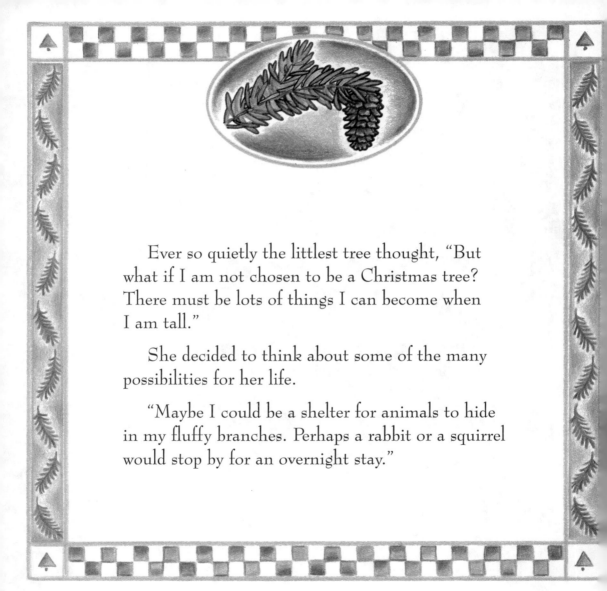

Ever so quietly the littlest tree thought, "But what if I am not chosen to be a Christmas tree? There must be lots of things I can become when I am tall."

She decided to think about some of the many possibilities for her life.

"Maybe I could be a shelter for animals to hide in my fluffy branches. Perhaps a rabbit or a squirrel would stop by for an overnight stay."

"Or I could be planted near a family's house and little birds will nest in my soft needles. I know my friends the chickadees would love to stay with me for the winter."

"They could fly from my branches to the bird feeders and window ledges and then fly back to me for safety."

The littlest tree was filled with ideas jumping from branch to branch as she thought about the many things she could become.

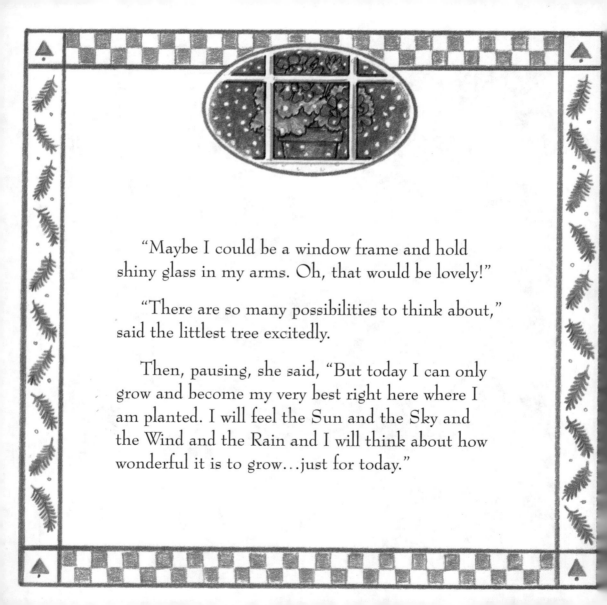

"Maybe I could be a window frame and hold shiny glass in my arms. Oh, that would be lovely!"

"There are so many possibilities to think about," said the littlest tree excitedly.

Then, pausing, she said, "But today I can only grow and become my very best right here where I am planted. I will feel the Sun and the Sky and the Wind and the Rain and I will think about how wonderful it is to grow…just for today."

The littlest tree often listened to the mother and father trees whispering with the other tall trees in the woods. They told stories of their ancestors, the giant old trees, so tall and majestic that even the strongest of men looked up at them with wonder.

Standing up as straight and tall as she could, the littlest tree stretched her tiny roots deep down into the soft, sandy soil.

She looked up to the Heavens and called out to her Creator,

"Invite the birds and the animals and all the people to come and walk between our rows of seedlings. Let them see the beauty of the Sky and the trees. Let them feel the magic of the Sun and the Wind and the Rain, and let them know the wonder of the forest."

At last, the littlest tree understood. The joy of being a Christmas tree can be found in each and every day.

Standing patiently in her row of seedling trees, The Littlest Christmas Tree looked up into the dark, starry night and whispered,

"Thank you, Dear Creator, for Life. Thank you for Dreams. Thank you for Ideas and Thoughts and Feelings. Most of all, thank you for choosing me to grow — just for today — and to know the Wonder of Your World and its many Possibilities."

About the Author

Janie Jasin is a nationally recognized motivational speaker who combines humor and enthusiasm with an uplifting message of affirmation. She is sought after by groups and organizations throughout the country for her unique ability to present life's challenges as positive growth experiences.

For information regarding permission, write to
Book Peddlers, 15245 Minnetonka Blvd., MN 55345-1510.
ISBN 0-439-13328-9
Text copyright © 1996 by Janie Jasin.
Illustrations copyright © 1996 by Book Peddlers.
All rights reserved. Published by Scholastic Inc.,
555 Broadway, New York, NY 10012, by arrangement with Book Peddlers.

SCHOLASTIC and associated logos are trademarks and/or registered
trademarks of Scholastic Inc.

12 11 10 9 8 7 6 5 4 3 2 1   9/9 0 1 2 3 4/0
Printed in the U.S.A   23

Pen and
colored
pencils
were used for all the
color art in the book.
The typeface
is Bernhard Modern